Lake Lonely

SHIRES PRESS

Manchester Center, VT 05255

Lake Lonely

ISBN: 978-1-60571-499-8 Paperback edition

ISBN: 978-1-60571-500-1 Hardcover edition

Lake Lonely

By Sue Jeffreys

Dedicated to

my Gramp

my favorite storyteller,

who gave me the gift of words.

Joseph P. Tarantino, Sr

Foreword

"Saratoga is like a fond memory. Once you are enticed by her charms, you will never forget her."

-Peter Finley, 3rd generation Saratogian,
Published local poet, Yaddo Garden Association Volunteer

"For this Saratogian, there is nothing better
than watching your handiwork rest on the withers of a
Champion"

-Susan Lee Garrett, Champion Floral Blankets by Susan,
Wishing Well Restaurant family member

"As a native Saratogian and photographer, I have always loved the Saratoga Race Course. I treasured my annual visits with Mr. Tarantino, a highlight of the season. He shared his old stories about Saratoga and taught me how to handicap."

-Elizabeth Macy, author, 'Lucky's Adventures'

"I grew up in downtown Saratoga. My grandmother would babysit us during the summer. One of the great memories was walking straight up Caroline Street, making our way to the Oklahoma Track to feed the horses sugar cubes. The West Side was where my Grandfather lived who they called 'King of the Hill' because he lived right at the top of Congress and Franklin Street."

-James Parker, 3rd generation.

About this Book

I read a quote once which literally summed up my heartfelt gratitude I feel for this town that I am honored to be a part of:
"If Saratoga didn't actually exist, it would have to be invented."
For me, Saratoga Springs is a hometown with all the comfy and cozy, yet it embodies all the joy feels a vacationland brings. It is a hard sell to get me to leave this town the minute Racing Season begins. Natives and tourists are drawn to the air of excitement, the tingles, the litany of gathering. We basically worship it. So, I began writing this novella a few years ago as a love letter to this beloved destination city, but recently it became more than that. Due to the significance of the 2020 pandemic, we have all gone back to cherishing the simple things. This has stirred up the universal theme of human connection, just like during post WWII which is the setting of the book. Isn't that what is most important to all of us? Connection. With that said, I truly hope that you enjoy this tiny, little story that has a big heart. It means so much to me to share it.

It is a journey piece- a journey of hope with touches of humor. Go out and find your laughter.
Go find your connection. Go find your joy.
And most of all, be grateful for the moments.

With love to all the readers,
Sue Jeffreys, Author

"The sun to rule the day…

The moon and the stars to rule the night."

Psalm 135

How can I then return in happy plight.

That am debarred the benefit of rest

When day's oppression is not eased by night,

But day by night and night by day oppressed?

And each, though enemies to either's reign,

Do in consent shake hands to torture me,

The one by toil, the other to complain

How far I toil, still farther off from thee.

I tell the day to please him thou art bright,

And dost him grace when clouds do blot the heaven.

So flatter I the swart-complexioned night, When

sparkling stars twire not, thou gild'st the even. But

day doth daily draw my sorrows longer, And night

doth make nightly grief's length seem stronger.

-Shakespeare

Prologue

Down the well-worn path rode the dark colored sedan, meandering through the midnight hour. The moon rose high in the sky, illuminating the tops of the pine trees. The road remained blackened as the wheels spun round and round in the muddy sludge. Clickety clop, clickety clop- was the only sound heard for miles around as the headlights barely exposed the trodden way. The inhabitants of the jagged vehicle sat in silence of their thoughts on this Saturday evening, transfixed on the hypnotic sound of the Studebaker's wheels going round and round. Every so often the bumps and valleys in the dirt road jarred them into the present reality of what their destination was. "Knowing was better than not knowing," rang repeatedly in Moe's head. Moe and Izzy were strong armed bookends in the backseat on each side of Nicky B, who was slumped over in prayer saying "Hail Marys" over and over again in a low chant that began to get under Izzy's skin. He pointed his elbow into Nicky Bricco's ribcage and pushed hard with a punishing force, hoping he would shut him up. Nicky continued his own conversation of prayer knowing that this was his only hope.

The daunting rain throughout the daylight hours had finally stopped but left a low hung fog as the night approached and the thickness was just beginning to recede as the temperatures went down. Humid did not even begin to describe this years' Northeast summers' wrath. Shady refuge in a lounge chair under the trees was the usual respite during peak sun hours. A pitcher of iced cold lemonade sat on every kitchen countertop as a way to cool off and refresh from the seasons heat. Nicky B. had that vision of his mother's blue pitcher of homemade squeezed lemons, sugar and water just waiting for him as the screened door of his childhood home banged shut behind him when he would visit. The dripping, cold condensation and that damn screen door that he never got around to fixing for his mother Mae B. "Hail Mary, full of grace…oh geez! What a fucking asshole I am," he said out loud. "Fuck, fuck, fuck!" he lamented and looked upwards as if he was swearing to the heavens.

That jolted Moe and Izzy to jump, startled off their seat. "What the fuck?" said Moe, as Izzy retorted, "SHUT THE FUCK UP?"

"Jump Jive Hep Hep" was blaring on the radio, "Come on boys let's have a ball…" Big Vic, the driver, was tapping to the music on the steering wheel to the rhythm of Cab Calloway's beat, "the jip-jam-jump is a jumpin' jive." He was oblivious to the exchange going on behind him.

The sound of the band echoed Calloway's jive as the party revelers descended from their cars heading into the double art deco doors. Behind the doors was a world of decadence and hedonism. A world where the common man became assuredly self-important for the night. Walking in, one felt like royalty, as maître d Peter would call out, 'Sir or Madam, may I escort you to your table." It was the start of the summer horse season and the air was full of frenzied anticipation only equal to that of Christmas Eve. On the weekend before the Saratoga Racetrack opening, the first summer after the war, the hepster place to be was on the outskirts of town. Along the dark shore of Lake Lonely, were gambling houses shining their light calling out to anyone who needed an escape from the routine of the day.

The fireflies in the willows marsh above the lake were zapping with lightening force as if to the beat of the music. The orchestra was always one of a huge national talent and would never disappoint. Ladies in high heels were clicking to their own rhythm on the flagstone walkway leading into Riley's Lakehouse. Peter greeted

each guest as they excitedly hurried to get to their table
near the dance floor. Tonight there was a kinetic buzz in
the air more so than usual. A stirring, a restlessness
permeated the air.

The wind was swirling the hems of the ladies' dresses
as they walked under the open aired portico.

There was already a line forming at the doorway at the
entrance. Expensive and cheap perfume filled the air,
allowing for a dizzy mishmash of fragrance blend. The
rain made it so that all the patrons were pressed up
closely to each other. Gleefully gathering, this had the
effect of camaraderie and conversation.

The night brought with it a heaviness not only in the air but a feeling inside that something was lurking, something was pressing but not releasing. The shallow existence of most of the bar's inhabitants took on a comedic parody of a one act play. The cast of characters each acted their roles with as much drama one would expect from these phony baloney social climbers. Marie Bricco was a regular at this watering hole. If it wasn't for the light, toe tapping melody being played in the corner by the house piano player, the air would have been the same inside as it was outside. She breathed in deeply then exhaled out the memory of her son's shenanigans as it quickly focused her attention on the melody of the "jumpin jive."

The piano player at the Spuyten Dival was a tall, lanky man with grayish hair at the tips and a beard to match. Jimmy Jazz use to play at The Cotton Club back in the 30's in Harlem. His face was one of those faces that the eyes lit up when you would talk to him. Marie B. yelled over to him as she was ordering her drink at the bar, "Hey Mr. Jimmy, how goes it?" He threw up his hand in a friendly wave then continued to play his tune. She strolled over and stood by his side, resting her arm on the top of the maple piano and she pushed her back to lean against the wall. She started to drum the beat on the piano top while he played the scat melody. She leaned in and said into his ear, "I like your shirt?" He said, "Come again?" She said it louder, "I LIKE YOUR SHIRT! Your Shirt!" while tugging at his collar. He grinned back just teasing her to say it repeatedly, "It's the kind that stays cool. The kind that breathes. You know us cool cats, Mae, we have to stay cool!" He began to play faster with a proud look on his face, grateful for their friendship. Grateful to someone even for a kind word on this scorcher of an evening.

On these hot summer nights, a moment of diversion was essential to keeping up the spirit. Mae was just happy to be out on the town. It was a tiny little spot, although it felt BIG to her, tucked away on a small street a few blocks from the big Racetrack and great little stop off on the way home from the bigger nightclubs out by the lake. She had been worrying about her son all day.

She ran out of prayers. So the next best thing was some music and imbibe to try to defrazzle her frazzled nerves. The music was soothing her. She felt pretty, all dressed up. Mr. Jimmy said, "You are a fine dinner, Mae B." With that she smiled a huge grin. She gave him a wink. They always had each other's back. Rare in the decade after Prohibition and recent unrest of World War II. Swaying back and forth while balancing her Kir Royale, she started to feel the beat. Tapping her foot. Snapping her fingers. She began a slow stride out onto the wooden dance floor. She shouted out to anyone who was in ear shot, "Let's do this boys!" As the piano player took a break, the juke box clicked on and flipped the record from its slot, the sultry voice of Lena Horne began to belt out "Stormy Weather." Mae swayed her hips to the smooth sound, "Don't know why there's no sun up in the sky…" Mr. Jimmy Jazz as he stood watching, he thought to himself, "A fine, fine dinner, for sure."

1

The screened door blew open from the gust of wind in the morning light of summer. Mae had been up late the night before worrying about her son, Nicholas Bricco. "Was he ever going to fix that screen on the damn swinging door?" she thought to herself. "Where had he been all week?" As she poured her first cup of strong, black coffee she sighed in release. She was feeling a little woozy from her fun night out and she said out loud, "My Lord, please watch over my numbskull of a son. God, only You know the extent of his ways. Keep him safe and if it is not too much trouble, make him change his socks at least weekly." She chuckled at the image of the last request as she gulped down a swig from her chipped white mug.

This past weekend had been a trying one full of tugs and pulls. "Why is it on these hot summer nights there are hot summer life swirls?" she offered out, but no one was there to listen. She washed the last of the breakfast dishes. She laid them on the drying rack. Sunday morning was normally reserved for church and then she would come home to prep and cook Sunday family dinner. It was a sacred ritual. Her way of keeping a moment. She was the self -designated Keeper of Moments. "Without moments what the hell was life about?" she thought. Again she sighed, wondering why she even bothered. And then another laugh sneaked out at the vision of her family sitting around the old wooden table, all talking at the same time, while trying to shove Gram's recipe old world meatballs recipe with Sunday sauce into their mouths. "Love," she thought, "Love is in the food." And with that, she went to get dressed for Mass.

She always liked to get there twenty minutes early to grab her favorite pew. It had the best view of Father Murphy at the pulpit when he gave his weekly sermon. She would nod at his preaching about service to others. She would nod when he spoke about the awareness of people needing people. But when he would start the preaching about guilt of sin, she would sit there just looking straight ahead. And Father Murphy would glance over, waiting for her approval and pausing in silence. But no nod would be offered by Marie B. Her mind would wander back to the days of restless moments. "Temporary loss of reason," she would justify it with. It was then that she would say in silence, "Please God forgive me as I did not know what the fuck I was thinking!" Then she would make sure she stuffed an extra dollar into the offering box as she exited church. Somehow in some small way, she thought it made up for her self-proclaimed sins.

Today she was going to get to the bottom of why her son did not come by to fix her front door and she herself would give him a sermon or two. She stood at the door and proceeded to head out to bring the light of day into her heart. "Sunshine cures all that ails you," she lamented. She set off to get her seat. As she walked down the sidewalk, she heard that door slam shut and she shuddered, rolled her eyes and said in a loud shrill, "HOLY HELL!! Why do I even bother?"

2

Knock Knock Knock…

"Open up!"

Knock Knock Knock…

"OPEN UP I SAID!"

Sergeant Franklin shouted louder and louder until his throat was hoarse. He banged harder and harder until his hand was throbbing. The magnificent ten foot, hardwood door on the top of the steps at The Chicago Club on Woodlawn Avenue, was standing in front of him almost calling out with warning, "Good luck trying to get past me." The peak window finally opened up to a dark brown eye glaring at him. He could feel the look of disdain searing into him from the person whom the eye was attached to. "What in crazy hell are you making this raucous about? Don't you realize it is 8 am in the morning? We are in the middle of a tense, all night poker game, that you are making more tense with your pounding," said the person attached to the bloodshot eyeball. "For the love of the Lord, come in you damn crazy fool!", he said while shaking his head as if a poker game was a normal happening at the crack of dawn.

Sergeant Francis Franklin tiptoed across the wooden floor while it creaked every few steps. He took off his hat respectfully and held it to his chest to keep honor with The Big Boss. He entered the room in the back of the parlor. In front of him was a gathering of men standing watch around a card table with two men seated on bentwood chairs. Each of the poker players were bleary eyed and disheveled, with shirts untucked and sleeves rolled up. Yet both were pinpoint focused on their next move. "I will raise you a thousand and match your thousand." said one guy. "Show me what you got…, the other guy started to say. Sergeant Francis Franklin interrupted as both men let out a sigh, "Your sister has been calling everywhere looking for you. Your nephew is not around and she has no idea where he is. She finally saw my wife and me at mass as we were walking in. I left them on the steps of the church and told them I would run over here to see if I could find you." Salvatore Cornica put his finger to his lips to shush up his close friend Francis as he said "I will be right with you, Frankie."

Sal and Frankie. Frankie and Sal. Buddies since grade school, both grew up on the West Side of town. Both cut from the cloth of immigrant families that descended upon Ellis Island from over The Pond. One from Cobh, Ireland. The other from Bari, Italy. Both seaport towns. Somehow these two men were destined to grow up side by side. Yet one was on the right side of the law and the other on the wrong side of the law. But they somehow made it work. Their relationship was one of mutual respect. Both had each other's back, no matter. In their tree fort as kids, that connected their childhood backyards, they made up a solemn pledge they used on the daily. They combined it from both their grandmothers' kitchen wall plaque blessings. "Until we meet again, may God hold you in the palm of His hand.

Ti Amo." Then they would tap each other's fists top to bottom, to seal the pledge. They did this still as adults each time they left each other. Both would belt out a laugh after at the vision of two grown men being two young kids again.

After the game broke up, the two friends walked outside to discuss todays' debacle. Sal was in a huffy at losing to The Big Boss as Frankie tried to diffuse the situation, "You know there is a lot of sadness in the world. This ain't one of them." That always brought Sal back from the edge. Sal was the dreamer and Frankie was the realist. 'Let's focus on some real stuff. Where the hell is your dumbass nephew? Mae is beside herself with worry." Frankie assessed. Sal had a deep feeling gnawing at him. It did not seem good.

Nicky was his pride and joy but additionally he was still green at The Business. Sal owned a fruit and vegetable store that was, how he put it, "Not Just for Apples and Peas." He and Frankie continued walking, took a right up Division Street to go figure this out at the store. They would get to the bottom of it as if it was the last thing they ever did.

3

The Empire Fruit Company was the legacy of Sal and his hope was to pass it down to his nephew. It was his own father's wish that it would continue to be a family run store when Sal took it over but his nephew had highfalutin aspirations to get a college degree in business. "Street smarts, that's all ya need." Sal would tell him weekly. Nicky would shrug him off.

The Cornico Family started their journey from Italy when Sal was 8 years old. Before they set out on The Carpathia, his grandmother kissed him farewell on the forehead and told him, "There were chocolates in the streets of America. Go find them, Sallie." Sal strived for those "chocolates' every working day. As a kid, he envisioned plucking the candy off bushes and eating them. But now he understood her words literally. He became part of the American Dream coming out of The

Depression years ago with high hopes. There was money to be made with hard work and it had paid off.

As he walked through the store into the back room to his office, he paused in reverence at the floor to ceiling bank safe where he put in the rest of the cash leftover from the card game. Every time he would turn that lock and hear the click, he felt like it was the sound of success. But his dumbass nephew didn't get it, he thought. "Where the hell was he?" Sal screamed out. Frankie was at the front counter talking to Jimmy Jazz. Jimmy stopped in each morning to grab his newspaper along with fresh peaches and a hand melon. Frankie and Jimmy gave each other the all-knowing look of, "Oh boy! Sal is in that mood again!"

Jimmy Jazz was squeezing the cantaloupe hand melons one by one. Smelling them so as to get the one with the perfect ripeness. "What Dear God are you doing? Let's go grab some breakfast and figure out a plan", said Sal. 'We need to get some eggs, bacon and hash in my belly before I can think." Jimmy, Frankie, and Sal started out walking down the street headed for the Colonial Tavern on Broadway. What a sight they were! Lanky, dark skinned Jimmy in the middle, with a cool, relaxed stride. Freckled Frankie, upright and straight with a confident walk. And then there was pasty white Sal, puffing and waddling, shirt still untucked, his dark hair uncombed, looking like a homeless man who just rolled out from the corner halfway house.

Mae and Kat were coming down Broadway from mass in their Sunday finest. "Ow!" Jimmy Jazz belted out at the sight of the two ladies. Kat Franklin ran over to her husband, Frankie and gave him a kiss on the cheek. Mae gave Jimmy a quick foxy stare, which became a scowl as she turned to her older brother and said, "What the heck time did you roll in, Sallie? I have been trying to call you before church!" "I got in at 8 chimes this morning." Sal returned with a mischievous grin. "Well, you sure look like you're melted out." she went on. Sal cut her off, "No gravy to be had at the card game. So let's go get us some grease. I need me some fuel to jump start my thick skulled idea pot. You're buying." All five of them gave out a huge roar of laughter as they walked in.

4

The Colonial Tavern was packed with after church goers that is except for Sal, who never went to church except for funerals and weddings. That even in itself was a big effort but he believed in family and friendship. That trumped all to him. So he would attend those church happenings and avoid eye contact with that giant stained glass window of Saints staring down above the altar, as if judging him. He followed his own spiritual mantra. Kindness and respect with an added boost of strong armed ambition, were his main commandments. He tried to be a good man but he always thought, "Don't fuck me over with disrespect!" That was his religion. "Sal's Creed," he called it.

The five close friends squeezed into one of the booths near the back. The clink of dishes and the smell of fresh brewed coffee was in the air. Sal waved over to the booth across from them. Monty Woolley and Frank Sullivan both nodded back yet kept focused on their chit chat. Both were barbing each other on some literary, yet most definitely salacious topic, trying to outsmart the other with their wit. One an actor of wit. The other a writer of wit.

Sal recalled a moment he had with these two guys as they were local and national celebrities. Both loved this town. It was in the depth of their beings. Especially August in Saratoga! Who could resist? Their humor was what drew Sal to them one late night at The Worden Hotel. It was a nice respite from the crowds on Broadway situated on the corner of Division Street. The red rug within, decorated with golden horseshoes gave it a warm welcoming feeling. Sal would tap the horseshoe imprints with each foot for good luck at the beginning of every August in hopes he would have some winners trackside. The bar was located below the hotel under street level and it was a meeting spot for regulars during the week who just wanted a bit of connection. Sal and Frankie would go midweek to catch up. One night they heard Monty say to Frank Sullivan, "I am a film actor but here in Saratoga I am just me. The flickers are magical of course, but this town, this place is pure magic particularly in racing season. It makes me happy. It is my home." The horse season was vital to the mind and spirit. This was inherent truth. Both men had houses in Saratoga and had found contentment in them.

That very same night Dorothy Parker walked in as she was Algonquin Table buddies with Frank Sullivan. She had a writer's residence at the Yaddo but was bored as hell on those solitary grounds. As she glided in she yelled over to Monty and Frank, "Hey, you two-Happify me! I need some fun. Order me a Gin Ricky, Let's get oiled!" Monty patted the bar stool and said, "Cop a squat right between us." Frank asked, "How's it going sassy lady?" "Well, you boys know me well," Dorothy continued as she recited one of her poems,

"The sun's gone dim and

The moon's turned black;

For I loved him, and

He didn't love back."

Then Dorothy asked them, "What do you two mugs have to say for yourselves?" Frank and Monty looked at each other, smiled, and in unison yelled out, "Ditto, Dottie!" All three of them clinked their glasses and the entire bar shouted, "Cheers to that!"

Sal and his breakfast crew laughed until their jaws hurt after he told this story. Sal was always the one who held everyone in his attention with the best tales. He had a way with detail. He was a good analyzer of people and would enjoy reiterating a fun story to anyone who would listen, embellishing the details.

As the five of them finished up their breakfast, Sal looked over at his sister Mae and held her hand. He completely adored her, gave her a self- assured squeeze of the hand as he thought, "I hope the sun hasn't gone dim for Nicky." Sallie grabbed the check as usual and gave the waitress a jolly smile and said, "Keep the change." He was always kind to people in service jobs. He knew they worked hard for every cent.

5

Jimmy Jazz was the first to say his good-byes, "I've
got to trilly along and head down for practice to tickle the
ivories for tonight's gig. I will keep my ears and eyes
open to any word on the street. See ya trackside, opening
day, under our favorite Elm trees in the paddock early
afternoon tomorrow. Give me a shout if you hear
anything." He gave Mae a quick wink as he sauntered
towards Phila Street. Mae smiled, then steadfastly
addressed her brother and close friends, "I say Kat and
Frankie, you go check out Congress Park while Sal
comes with me to The Hawley Home. We will meet back
at the store after, and head over towards Congress
Theater, if nothing comes to light in the meantime. See
you after in a jiffy."

Kat and Frankie walked down Broadway arm and arm
as Sal with Mae, took the left onto the Spring Street hill
adjacent to the park. Frankie was glad to have some alone

time with his sweetie on this bright Sunday morning. The sky was the deep color of blue with a few fluffy clouds floating by. The birds were chirping as Frankie looked over to his lovely wife, "You are my main queen, Kattie." "You know you are my guy, Frankie!" Kat tried to say with some ounce of enthusiasm to the husband she adored. Yet she was in worry mode. Kat usually was the pick me up girl, the lifter of spirits. She was Mae's closest friend and confidante. She felt Mae's sadness as if it was her own. "Where was Nicky B.?" she yelled out so fiercely, it made the gaggle of ducks crossing the walkway literally jump back in the pond. "Look at that!" said Frankie, "you literally just scared the shit out of the Mommy and her ducklings." he pointed to the sidewalk covered with poo. It broke the tension of the mystery at hand as both laughed until they had tears in their eyes. But no sight of Nicky anywhere as they scanned the park. They sat down on the bench overlooking the gazebo. This is where they had their first date back in the early 1930s. They had first seen each other across the library one early evening. She caught a glimpse of him and his

humorous demeanor. It was love at first glimpse. Frankie
was running away from an eager young lady literally
chasing him from the stacks of books. Kat was standing
at the card catalog with Mae and they giggled at the sight
of him running, ranting and raving about how there was
no sanctuary of peace to read even in a library! He ran all
the way out the front double doors onto Broadway. And
never looked back, still reciting his grievances to anyone
in ear shot, while proceeding into the park. Kat ran to the
full wall of windows in the back of the library to watch
this hilarious exchange of words Frankie was still having,
now with the ducks. He plopped himself on the bench
under the shade of the magical willow tree that stood at
the center of the pond. He cracked open his book. She
could see his broad shoulders finally relax. She let out a
sigh of relief in unison. Right then and there she knew
they were connected. Connected by the pull of the
universe in all its bigness. And at that single moment, she
vowed to continue this connection. She made her way
outside, sat next to him, and so they began.

6

Sal and Mae walked up the steps of The Hawley Home for Children. It was hard for Mae to think back to the day she dropped Nicky off here. He was a young boy of 8 years old during the start of The Great Depression and Mae was a struggling, single mother trying to juggle two jobs. One at an electronics shop, nights and weekends on Henry Street filling in for her no good, louse of a runaway husband. And the other where she was full time employed, The Van Raalte Knitting Mill on High Rock Avenue. Her brother's fruit and vegetable business was struggling then due to the distress of the economy. She was grateful to even have income at that time, for jobs were scarce. Due to the war, women were going into the work force to fill jobs men fighting for our country had vacated. She knew her son needed a refuge as she brought in the money to make ends meet. Hard decisions were vital so this orphanage home became her son's temporary sanctuary. A home away from home.

Hawley Home was her savior and Nicky's retreat. He never forgot what this place meant to him and his mother, so he vowed to give back in any way he could. Each Sunday morning as an adult, he would bring the current children fresh donuts and then would play a game of stickball on the lawn before he would head out. Every Friday afternoon during the school term months, "the kids" as he called them, would all sit around the radio in the recreation room off the front hall to catch the current episode of the serial Captain Midnight. The kids would recite the series mantra together as Nicky would speak in Captain Midnight's voice:

"Tolling of the bell, the roar of the plane, and its Captain Midnight."

They would all pretend they were on a high-risk mission, and hang onto every word of each episode. After, they would celebrate around the huge dining room table with Ovaltine milk and homemade peanut butter cookies. Clinking their glasses, reeling out sarcastically, "So good for you!" The slogan taken from the advertisement during the radio show. Each had their Ovaltine mailed decoder whistles in hand, laughing so hard the milk almost came out of their noses. Nicky B. loved these kids and they loved him.

"Well, hello to you my friends, Sallie and Mae. What do I owe this honor?" said Matron Maggie. "Have you seen Nicky around this weekend?" said Mae with a worried inflection in her voice. "Sorry to say, it's the first one he has ever missed." Maggie sadly responded. Sal said with great concern and frustration, "That's a bring down. If he stops in, please have my dumbass nephew call his Mama."

They walked out on the front porch both with grimaces on their faces. Mae glanced back over her shoulder at the huge brick building behind her as she descended on the walkway. She choked up and with tears in her eyes she waved to the children peering out the front parlor window. Her heart just about broke in half when

Sal put his arm around her to protect her from the memory of long ago. Both felt thankful there was this place watching over the forlorn, temporarily abandoned children in town.

Mae had asked her boss to take off opening day from her full time job at the Van Raalte Knitting Mill on High Rock Avenue. She was looking forward to it like every single inhabitant in this resort town. The mill had been closed for four years due to less demand for silk from The Great Depression. But it reopened, and they started making nylon hosiery. Nylon was the new miracle fabric and Mae was at the forefront of it's' explosion. She relished progress.

Their company slogan was-

"VAN RAALTE: Because You Love Nice Things."

And Mae sure did love nice things. But mostly she loved that this company gave her the opportunity to provide an income as a single mother to feed and clothe her son. Taking off the day was a much needed fun day for her and she had been planning out her new outfit. But now

with Nicky a no show, everything was starting to feel like
a down beat. She gave herself a pep talk, "Get in there,"
but all she felt was hung up.

7

The parade of horses that just came in off the morning train were in full sight as Sal and Mae walked up from Ludlow Street onto Union Avenue. The trains would arrive on the West Side with the horses on board coming in from various downstate trainers. People would come watch in droves at this display of arrival. It meant "The Horses Have Come to Town." They are ready to run as the season has begun. The boxcar doors would open and there were these magnificent creatures standing valiantly in stalls. Their groomers had them looking brushed and shiny. They would be led off the wooden planks from their journey outside of NYC. Every horse had a handler. From a distance Sal and Mae could see the exercise grooms holding the reigns of each horse walking behind the other. One by one in a row, they would cross over to Circular Street from West Circular and make their way to the Horse Haven barns adjacent to the training track.

Their manes were blowing in the breeze. Some chestnut, some bay, some grey. The clopping sound of their hooves created a musical beat as they paraded along. The horses would sing out with neighs as if saying, "We are back. Let's get this party started." "August, the month this old town sure does spring to life but it's so damn crowded." Sal muttered.

Union Avenue was just about the widest house and tree lined street in the city with the exception of North Broadway. Its origin had the honor of being situated at the top of Congress Park. It lead all the way past the black iron fenced entrance of Saratoga Racetrack and proceeded on its way to the stoned pillars of the fabled artists retreat, Yaddo and then continued out towards the lakes. During the summer season, this avenue was especially well- traveled with the hustle and bustle of a mix of tourists along with natives of the town. Sal was grumbling about how frenzied the town got this time of year, "It is no wonder this damn street is named Union. It intersects every fool who jumped into port. They are here to play the horses for a big win. Yah right! They are all

chalk players, anyway. But at least this town is jumpin!",
as he ran annoyed crossing from the corner of sidewalk to
the park. Yet in his heart, he felt proud of its horsey
history. "You know our town doubles in size in August?
Relax mixed with action. Yes sireee! You get the best of
both here, don't ya Mae? Mae? Are you there?" Sal
asked. Mae was lost in thought as she ignored his ranting,
resolve and review. She was use to Sallie's soliloquy
delivery which usually made her laugh but today was full
of intensity and focus. She needed to think. Her son's
absence was weighing on her. She had that mother's
sixth sense starting to kick in and it wasn't feeling fine.
Not fine at all. "Sallie, do you think something bad has
happened? I think we should swing by the electronics
shop and see if anyone has heard from him. Then we can
go over to Congress Theater and see if he is hanging out
at the movies or the snack bar. That is where all his
buddies go on Sundays to ward off their weekend
hangovers. It may be worth a try." Mae said calculating
some ideas as she and Sal walked through the center of
Congress Park. All Sal was thinking inside was, "I can't

wait to get my hands on that little punk and tell him a thing or two or three."

8

The electronics shop was located in "The Gut' of the city on Henry Street. "Get it at the Gut" was the slogan. They gave it this nickname because it was located in a low valley off Broadway. Basically, it was a front for alcohol sales during the Prohibition. It was an easy go to from Route 9 after a delivery run on the rum trail where they would bring back truckload cases of alcohol to store hidden in between the walls. But now it sold legit radios and cooling household fans, in addition to unloading "hot items" that were not so legit. Either way it was a hangout for discussing daily ramblings of politics and local gossip. A dishing of truth and untruths. Nothing got by this place without judgement by the panel of know it alls.

Dashing Dice. Billy the Pusher. Uncle Mike, the Ubiquitous Uncle Characters seemingly right out of a film noir casting call but a big hearted bunch.

Mae ended up working there part time so she knew this place well, filling in for her husband after he left town. Her ex-husband was all talk and no action. "A good looking, no good nothing," Mae would always describe him as. He worked for one of the Big Bosses in town as his right hand man, yet just never could get it together. In reality, he had big dreams that never amounted to a solid. One day she finally had enough. He would go on benders and drink for days. They couldn't find him one week when Nicky was a young boy. Finally, they did locate him in the basement of the electronics shop. He was in a cockpit fog from his daily drinking binges, sleeping it off on an old mattress below the store level. With Nicky missing now, it gave her pause that he was following in his father's footsteps but she quickly put that thought aside. He was not a wild drinker so it had to be for another reason. "But what was it? Where was he?" she thought. She and Sal decided this

might be the perfect place to find out. Information
central at The Gut. The spot of all spots to shoot the shit
and to grab the goods.

This current situation brought back the day Mae took
a stand. "The Last Straw That Broke the Camel's Back
Day," as she referred to it.   On that horrid day her
husband showed up on her doorstep but he didn't get past
the WELCOME doormat. Her brave, loud comeback was
not so welcoming which was expressed not only with
some harsh pointed words but also at the edge of a shiny
pointed knife. She said, "Get the hell outta here! Don't
you ever come back!" He knew that he better get up and
down out of there. He realized there was no fixing it this
time. He looked up at her with disgusted disillusionment
and she accepted the realization that he finally gave in.
The real of it was that he couldn't fix his demons. She
saw it in his eyes, sadness mixed with defeat. The best he
could do for his wife and son was to turn and walk away.
And that is what he did. He took the last bus out of town
back up to Malone, where she had first met him in a
coffee shop as a counter waitress. It was a heavy lard to

bare but in her usual style, she pulled herself up. "Chin up and walk forward," she thought. And so she bravely filled in for him that next day at the shop to occupy the spot her husband vacated. The guys had welcomed her with open arms like family. This put food on her table and clothing on her son's back. No self-pity, only self-preservation. The mantra of a mother.

As Mae and Sal walked into the shop full of friends, they asked the gang of guys if they had seen Nicky around. None of them had a clue where he was. This was disconcerting because if this big boy bunch of know-it -alls had no clue then no one did, being it was the towns information funnel center. Everything went through here. Nothing got past this crew. They were running out of ideas and Mae was in red alert worry mode. She looked at Sal with sadness in her eyes. But she took her own advice. She put her chin up and walked forward. They decided to go grab Kat and Frankie and head over near Congress Theater to find him or some of his buddies. She was hopeful like a mom always is. This was like a jigsaw puzzle journey of hope. They had to know. They just had to.

___

9

The main drag was getting a mix of Sunday Funday Frolickers. At the prominent corner of Spring Street and Broadway, Congress Theater sat in all its' majestic regal glory. A place to escape or a place to connect. Either way it provided a relief from the everyday routine of life. Couples in star dust mode would hold hands as they waited in line for the matinee, ready to get neck happy and nuzzle smooches in the back row. Moms and Dads dragging their sticky-handed kiddies from the concession stand. Single patrons who were self-proclaimed film connoisseurs buying their ticket to a weekend release movie. All this on a Sunday mid- afternoon, while Mae looked on thinking, "I wish I could sneak away and escape into this movie to get away from my gnawing feeling of distress." But it was hard for her to concentrate right now. Both Sal and Mae were waiting for Frankie and Kat to meet up to go inside the lobby area just to get

a look see on Nicky or any of his buddies. Sal was
chatting to one of his own pals standing in line who was a
jabber box, talking about the track reopening and singing
the theme song in barbershop chorus fashion, "Night and
Day. You are the one. Only you beneath the moon or
under the sun." Mae glared over to her brother, and with
a roll of her eyes said, "ARE YOU COMING SALLIE!"
Without one second of hesitation he saw and hurriedly
waved on Kat and Frankie and pointed to the entrance.
All four of them walked inside. Yet Mae paused and
looked up. The matinee movie on the marquee at the
forefront of the building, shown boldly in big dark letters
against the lighted, white background:

NIGHT and DAY

A Cole Porter Film

From Warner Brothers

Starring Cary Grant with Monty Woolley

Composer Max Steiner with Cole Porter

Saratoga's own home boy, Monty Woolley made an appearance as himself in the movie. So it fittingly was the perfect summer film that had a lot of the Saratoga flavor already attached to it. The musical was a much needed respite from the bright sun. Escaping into the darkened, cool theater to listen to Cole Porter's most enduring songs, was as good as it gets without actually making the three hour trek to live theater on Broadway in NYC. Instead, Broadway in Saratoga was the epicenter of tourist season and what a better way to celebrate the day prior to the track opening! Tickets for the evening performance were almost already sold out, so the afternoon showing was getting packed full of patrons begging for second choice leftovers.

The four close friends walked around checking the food counter, scanning the theater occupants sitting eating their popcorn, chair by chair. Nothing, not even one of his friends, "No go. No Nicky," Frankie and Kat said in unison. Sallie said, "Nicky and his buddies are probably hanging out on the beach by Kaydeross Park warding off their hangovers from this weekend." Mae told them, "If that's the case, let's just let him be. Maybe it was simply a bunch of his gang, planning out their strategies, sharing their rumpled up Daily Racing Forms in hand, trying to beat the books for tomorrow's race day card. Just maybe they were pooling five spots and dime notes for their scratch sheet handicapping. But whatever it is, I'm over this silly search. I have wasted enough of the day and so have all of you!"

In defeat and with a bit of apprehension, they all hugged it out. Walking back into the daylight, with painful squinting eyes because of the deep darkness inside the theater, they all went their separate ways with "see you trackside" salutations as they left.

Mae had to ready and prepare Sunday dinner. She started out walking back home on the West Side of town where all the streets were named after trees.

Oak Street. Ash Street. Birch Street. Interweaving to
form a neighborhood the occupants felt connected in.

Many of them immigrants. Many of them diverse of
color. A community of spirit, where living a life that
drew riches from hard work meant happiness for their
families. After The Depression and Prohibition, there was
a new sense of "no limits" on what one could accomplish.
Additionally, WWII added a longing for a calmness from
the simple things. The reemerging from discussing
economic and social issues provided a liberalism never
felt before. These discussions, while sitting on porches
after dinner were at the center of family life. This
common thread connect reinforced a stepping stone to
their dreams. A way of a life to be proud of.

Mae had taken tomorrow's big track day off from The
Van Raalte Knitting Mill. Her full time job gave her the
income to provide a house and a home so that her family
and friends could gather especially on Sunday. This gave
her a satisfied solace.

Sallie was shuffling along Broadway down to Division Street feeling not so proud of his nephew. He was grimacing with huffing and puffing, not noticing anything in front of him. He had to go back over to the store to ready it for closing time. He lived in a small apartment over the store. He would go grab a shower before heading over to Mae's for an early dinner. He had to go tend to his Victory Garden he planted in her backyard during the war years as a useful way to supplement rations. People planted these gardens also as a way to boost morale. Sal was always in need of a personality morale boost, that was for sure. In addition to the vegetables, he had planted a perimeter of bright blue larkspur flowers. They stood like a wall of protection he thought. Last fall, he got distracted and stupidly mowed half of them down. Mae just about cried but then she burst out laughing and said, "What am I going to do with you?" This spring he had replanted and they came back better than ever. The garden provided some escape. The routine tasks of midday would keep he and Mae focused and their mind from thinking the worst. As Sal hopped in the shower, he knew one thing for sure, talking to the steamed up mirror, wiping it with the bath towel, "Nicky B. WOULD NOT MISS OPENING DAY!"

THAT NIGHT

Lake Lonely at Midnight

The pearls around her neck felt cool in contrast to the warmth of the humid evening. She went to the open window to catch a breeze from the night air, but all she could feel was the stillness of the darkness outside. The crickets were singing the song of a summer night as she closed her eyes to feel the energy of their sound. As she walked out onto the back lawn of Rileys Lake House, she looked out over the marshes next to Lake Lonely. She herself was feeling lonely among the glittering guests who were in full party mode. It was stifling to her. All that chatter and laughter. She thought as she looked towards the lake, how muddy and cool that ground must be leading down the banks of the hill next to the water's edge. She wanted to feel the coolness on her bare feet. She ran towards the hill and paused to carefully take off her leather sandals and placed them next to a small tree. In the moonlight, she pulled her beaded dress over her head and let it fall to the ground. She stood for a moment in her silken ivory slip, listening to the peaceful silence. She could just barely hear the live orchestra inside the lake house. It was playing, "As Long as I Live" from last year's film, "Saratoga Trunk". Behind the walls inside Rileys, they were doing a special tribute on the eve of the racetrack opening. Earlier she had seen Max Steiner, the composer, sitting with Edna Ferber, the author, at the house table. The orchestra had begun playing it out of respect in their honor:

"As long as I live

You'll always be a part of me.

You'll live in the heart of me

As long as I live

As long as I love I'll share it with you, my own

And want to be loved by you alone

How sure am of all the things I say

As sure as night

Will fall at close of day

You're all that I need

So answer this love I give

And whisper "I'm yours"

As long as I live."

Edna and Max had worked together in the past on "Stage Door" then on "Saratoga Trunk." They had a bucket of bubbly on their table. With a loud clink and cheers, they toasted their success to each other with this wonderful tribute from the orchestra.

It was now past midnight. She could see in the distance the car valets, sharing a smoke. Passing a cigarette back and forth. They were filling time until the patrons were ready to depart. Joe's Taxi Cab sat pulled up at the entrance waiting for a fare pick up. She turned towards Lake Lonely and ran down the hill with abandon and restlessness.

Nicky B. had rowed and rowed until he could not row anymore. He got out of the boat to shore on the other side of the lake. He had placed the rowboat he just departed from under a small cluster of bushes and tied it to one of the branches. He had escaped those bozos Moe and Izzy after two days sequestered against his will, in a lakeside cabin. He had waited until those imbeciles were in a synchronized snoring symphony after a boozy game of dice. Nicky quietly crept out the back door. He had run in the darkness through the woods parallel to the water but stayed out of sight. He kept a small rowboat at a small dock down by the shore. He would go there on nights to contemplate his life but tonight he was on the run from his messed up life. How had he forgotten to make the drop off for the Big Boss? And where was the money now? He did these side jobs to sack away money for his business school fund. But he made a dumb ass decision to be involved with this bunch of low life greedy bookie degenerates. Now it all was falling apart until this very moment as he stood still in silence, watching.

He wanted to look away and give her some privacy but he could not resist. Her hair glistened from the moon reflecting off the water. It was as if there was a spotlight on this beautiful being. It energized every sense in him. He closed his eyes to save the image and at that very moment all he could think, "SO GOOD FOR YOU!' He burst out laughing at the Ovaltine mantra and tripped over a rock. She heard a rustle across the way yet did not see him. She thought it was a turtle splashing in. She walked to the waters' edge. Muddy squishy squash was oozing between her toes. She felt the release of the suffocation seep out of her pores. Inhaling and then deeply exhaling. The cool darkness of the lake wrapped around her like a fresh cleaned bedsheet. The moonlight was still on her as Nicky watched this waltz with nature. It was almost too much for him. The kinetic force of this moment caught him off guard to the point of holding his breath. He watched as she twirled around and around in the knee depth water. She then stopped, bowed and blew a kiss to the stars. Then made a pivot, walked back up the hill and disappeared out of sight into the night.

Lily ran and she ran, all the way up the hill. The night breeze made her shiver as she felt the dampness of her clothing stuck against her skin. The air was still warm but the water had brought her the coolness she needed to relieve her. She grabbed her dress, took off the wet slip and left it hanging on the tree branch to dry. She was standing there still under the moonlight, as she placed her dress over her naked body. With her sandals in hand, she walked barefooted by the jaw dropped valets starring at her, straight into the backseat of the taxicab. She rolled down the back window and said to them, "Hot and Bothered! The youth of today are so hot and bothered. Go find yourselves some fun," as she blew each of them a kiss and winked to Joe in the mirror. "Hi Joe! How's the evening going for ya?" and without pause, "Please bring me to the barns of Horse Haven." She needed to go oversee the 5 a.m. prepping of her filly. This is where she always found a wholeness and an inner peace, with the horses. This is where she felt home.

Cabby Joe was the keeper of secrets. At this time of night, he saw it all. He kept the secrets with guarded confidence, never gossiping, always advising. He was the taxicab soother of souls. His passengers would talk to him about their innermost thoughts. He would nod and listen with that twinkle in his blue eyes. That soothing color of greenish blue sparkled as he put his foot on the pedal and the cab sped off while Lily looked pensive out the window.

Nicky B. was still hanging on the shore, trying to process the jolt he just experienced. He also began to talk out loud to make sense of all the nonsense of the last two days. Standing at the water's edge he looked like a tragic hero in a Shakespeare play delivering a soliloquy, yet his words were not as poetic,

"Who the fuck am I?

What the fuck am I doing here?

Where the fuck am I going?

When the fuck am I going to learn?

Why the fuck am I a dumbass?

How the fuck am I getting out of this?"

He thought to himself in sarcastic disbelief, "Wow
that is brilliant, Nicky. You sure do have a handle on
NOTHING!" He stood there like a beaten down nobody.
His head lowered into his hands, he began to rub his scalp
as if to start some circulation to trigger his brain into
brilliance. Rubbing and rubbing until he felt a burn. He
looked up to the stars and saw the Big Dipper and the
Small Dipper close to each other and it reminded him of
him and his Uncle Sal. For a brief minute he had a warm,
heartfelt feeling. Then he thought in despair, OH NO,
THE BIG DIPPER. The Big Bear, Uncle Sallie! Sal is
going to be ready to give me a piece of his mind. I better
get moving"

Daybreak was not far away. August in Saratoga
begins at the crack of dawn. It wasn't out of the ordinary
that someone would be walking on the side of the road at
this early hour. Nicky B. was full of adrenaline. The two
miles from Lake Lonely up onto Union Avenue towards
town was not a drudgery at all. It started to feel like a
journey of hope. The lightbulb finally went off for him.

He was going to face his Uncle Sal with the strength of an adult.

He was 24 years old and he was ready to hit the quarter of century mark at the end of this month. It was time for him to "Grow the fuck up!" as Uncle Sallie would chime in his ear daily. "I am ready for this. A new day. A new way." as Nicky thought, "August 5, 1946 is the day I make my mark."

But right now he had to figure out how he was going to find the bag of cash the bookies, Moe and Izzy had entrusted him to make on the weekend drop off from Sal's safe to The Arcade Building on Broadway. This is where Moe and Izzy had an Insurance Agency that basically was a front for their bookie business. Sal was their trusted acquaintance, a confidante who was only involved in the convoy of cash. He let them store it in his safe until they needed it for the weekend book of numbers. Every Friday evening at midnight Nicky was in charge of making the trek to transfer from one place to the other for the drop off. But this past Friday somehow he forgot to carry out his duties. When the guys got wind of his blunder they thought he was on the lamb to steal the cash. They found him at the corner bar Saturday with his buddies, Lenny Valvano and Drew Guiffre. They were planning their Monday opening day happening at the track. The whole town was buzzing and jibber jabbering about it because of its temporary closure for the past three war years. This was a celebration weekend to gear up with anticipation. Everyone was on full throttle party mode.

Except for Moe and Izzy, who were on a rampage of recovery. When the pair of bookies walked into The Worden Bar, they said to Nicky, "We need to talk!" arms clasped on each side of him, grabbed and walked him to the waiting car in the back alley. They sped off into the darkness. Lenny and Drew looked at each other, shrugged their shoulders and figured it was just a normal night in Nicky's world.

As he continued his journey on Union Avenue, Nicky was walking out of the darkness into the dawn of day. He began to think how he had escaped their wrath with a brilliance he had never felt before. The stone pillars at the entrance of Yaddo were daunting at this hour. The ghosts of past artists and writers seemed to walk these hallowed grounds. But he decided to enter anyway because he knew a shortcut nearby that connected this property to the back side of the racetrack. He had significant feels for this sacred place. He spent a lot of time there.

Nicky as a young boy would go here with his Uncle Sallie. One standout time was a cold winter afternoon, when Sal got the bright idea to attach a wooden pull sled they had borrowed from The Hawley Home, to the back of his car bumper. He carelessly said, "Nicky, do you want to feel the glide of the snow covered road? Jump on the sled and I will drive the car." Nicky excitedly sat down on the wooden slatted sleigh as Sal yelled out the front window, "You ready Nicky boy?" He stepped on the gas pedal as Nicky was screaming with joy, "Faster, faster!" Sal was watching him from the rearview mirror when all of a sudden there was no Nicky in sight. Sal

thought, "Did that little whipper snapper jump off?" He
slowed down, stopped the car, and flew out of the front
seat and walked behind the car. There was Nicky semi
underneath the back bumper, sled and all. Nicky said
with a huge grin "That was fun. Let's do it again!" As
Sal pulled him out by his red wool hat he said, "Oh Boy,
your mother is going to scream my head right off. Lucky
for me you still have a head!" Nicky placed Sal's hand in
his and said, "Don't you worry Uncle Sallie, this is our
little secret. You and me, buddy up for the long run."

Nicky crossed over between the two ponds and was
remembering fondly that winter day on that very spot as
the sun greeted the dawn and it began to rise over the tall
pine tree line. Colors of orange and deep purple were
beginning to paint the sky. He walked over to the grass-
filled knoll, by the looming artist's mansion that was
staring down on him. He felt small looking up the hill at
this building made of stone but then he began to feel a
strength grow inside of him equaled to Yaddo's
magnificence. In this eerily dark woods with the light
peeking out on the horizon, he was ready to tackle the

world. He started his trek on the dirt path. "One step, then another. I got this fuckers!" he shouted to no one but the crows.

THAT DAY

Saratoga Racetrack Opening Day: August 5, 1946

*The women were all in ragout mode, dressed to the
nines. It was a super duper day to be seen in your
fashion finery. The men went all out, too. Dapper Dans
with hats on their heads and cigars dangling from their
mouths. Patrons carried the local newspaper, The
Saratogian with the headline in bold letters announcing,
"Crowds Jam City for Return of Racing," and The New
York Post touting the small bettors with their lead story,
"Two-Buckers Crowd Spa." It was a glorious day of all
kinds of bettors with a boodle of cash in their pockets
parading in, returning after a three year hiatus due to
WWII rationing and closures.*

*The town had been in a holding pattern for those
three summers and felt the economic loss along with the
loss of spirit. Summer Saratoga gatherings were based
around this ritual. With its closure, it left a gaping black
hole in the social gathering pot. The gear up to August
had lost its momentum until this reopening. The light
revelry had descended upon the day and the excitement
was contagious. Five thousand people stood in line early
to get in for the eight race card that started at 2:30 p.m.
on this Monday to enjoy a full afternoon of horsey
happenings. Fun was on everyone's mind with a unified*

conviction, looking to take part in this celebration that brought in more than fifteen thousand people on the track grounds. Opening day was back to stay. The people needed this summer venue because it was a ritual that was etched into their souls. Without it, they didn't feel the same. They felt out of sorts. The magic was missing. Not to mention the economic impact it had. There was no doubt that it felt normal to be back again, together at this unified gathering.

In the New York Herald Tribune, it stated that "There are bigger racetracks than Saratoga, but there is none like it." This was no more apparent just by watching the way the track goers were rushing in to get to their favorite spots. The birds in the elm trees surrounding the paddock also seemed to be singing a tune of celebration. Mae and Sallie were hanging by the Clubhouse entrance as Jimmy Jazz strolled in after handing over his $1.60 admission fee and said to Mae, "Look at you, pure aces today!" Sal and Jimmy hugged it out. Their deep friendship bond seeping out between them, then stepped back and did the fist on top to bottom handshake. Jimmy with his warm grin said, "Flip the grip, my main man." Mae screeched out in sarcasm, "You two bums, let's get over to The Jim Dandy Bar before it gets crowded. I need to get my spot front and center at the bar before all those hussies try to make their moves on both you guys." They began walking up the path leading into the Clubhouse, Mae in the middle with her arms entrenched *in both men's arms. She looked at each of them out of the corner of her eyes and thought to herself, "I am one lucky lady!" but deep in her mind all she was thinking about was her son's whereabouts.*

They entered The Jim Dandy Bar under the big red lettered sign and saw Kat and Frankie talking to the bartender, Tony Maloni. He came in from the New York downstate tracks to work seasonally in Saratoga and they were in deep conversation as they all saw each other. "Hey to my Saratoga Sunshine Gang! From the sounds of it, all of you need a drink to calm what ails you. What can I get you? Give it to me straight and unravel the gravel with some gossip." He was the singing bartender and started belting out, "I'm always chasing rainbows, watching clouds drifting by." Sallie interrupted him in mid tune, "Stop the baloney Tony Maloni. Have you seen Nicky come in today, maybe with a girlfriend?" He gave Sallie a look over his horned rimmed eyeglasses and said, "I've only seen him with that guy that limps. I've never seen him with a woman." Nicky's normal opening day routine was to walk into the bar with the old guy after buying programs at the stand. But today there was only the guy with the hobble leg at the other side of the Jim Dandy Bar. Tony and Sal gave him a wave and salute as he was an old war veteran. Nicky had typically made a point to pay at the program stand for this old fella he had befriended each opening day and then would get him his first round of drinks. It was their usual ritual that they had been doing for years since Nicky was old enough to drink at this famed bar. "I guess it was a no go today!" Tony said as Kat, Frankie, Mae all were talking at the same time. Sal muttered something unintelligible under his breath but no one there recognized what he was saying. It was more like two words flip flopped backwards made into one. "JibberJabber or GabbleGather," they thought Sal said, all red in the face, shaking his head in frustration. He just couldn't deal with all the mingling of talking. Tony Maloni set their old fashioneds lined up in front of them and said, "Don't get yourselves in a huffy. Nicky is probably on a quest with a lovely lady. You know, lipstick has gotten more men in trouble!" All of them looked at each other and Sallie held up his glass and muttered, "Hey pour man, that's for damn sure!"

At the other end of the bar was Anthony, nicknamed Shimali because he always smiled. Sallie and Shimali. He was one of Sallies buddies from the North End of Boston. He had his cigar in his hand that he never lit and his scaly cap on his head that he never took off. They shared a friendship that went back to the days of ending Prohibition. Both were young adults starting out on the new era of upswing. They had met down at The Gut, where he would drop off radios. He was somewhat like a wholesale middleman of "hot items." They hit it off from the moment they met. Toughies on the outside with big soft hearts on the inside. They had a common kindness thread in them as they both took care of those that fell on hard times. Anthony would go to The Home for Little Wanderers every Christmas to drop off toys to the orphans just like Sallie would bring gifts to the Hawley Home for kids when Nicky was there. Both had a strong work ethic. Both put family and friends first. Yet don't mess with either one of them as they were strong in spirit, so to speak and very passionate about their life "creeds." Determination and resolve of a bear and a bull. Sallie walked over to the other side of the full roomed walled bar and huddled up next to his buddy for a 'business' chat, to inquire how it was going on the streets of the North End. They gave each other a long, hard hug. They talked dealings and enterprises. They continued to chat baseball. One a Yankees Fan, the other a Red Sox guy. Rivals in sports. Friends always.

These guys just came out of WWII with the conviction of the American Spirit. During that time there was rationing and new lifestyle changes. Jobs were lost and there were many just trying to survive putting food on the table. This is where these two men stepped up. Sal's fruit and vegetable business was a go to for many families trying to feed their children. Anthony was keeping product moving through Beantown. Even though he sold "hot stuff", he took care of the nuns and priests in that small neighborhood not to mention paying off the cops to look the other way. Economics with heart and soul. Both men got it right as both were comrades of the success story and both were productive pushers. Sallie said his goodbyes and good luck wishes. He yelled over to the fun bunch, "Let's get to our box for the start of the race. I have to go make my bets and will meet you upstairs." Sallie had gotten a box for this celebration occasion from a guy who knew a guy. He walked over to the tote board and gave a nod to a woman in white walking past him with a long stride of determination and designation. He shook his head and thought to himself, "Why is everyone always in a hurry at this track? Where are they going? Everyone seems to have a hurry up to get nowhere attitude." The mutual clerk looked at him with disgusted angst and frustration as if to say, "Hurry up!" Sallie just looked at him with the same question and said out loud, "Hurry up to go nowhere!" And began listing his list of bets for the first race. "Buddy, I am just here to do my job. Just give me your bets." The mutual clerk rolled his eyes with impatience and mundane indifference.

As she walked by, Lily LaMont top to bottom, clothing, hat, jewelry, shoes, all in white, strutted across the ground floor of the clubhouse heading over to the wooden staircases that led up to the box seating area which overlooked the finish line. She was a horse owner from a long line of successful horse owners. Her filly, MIDNIGHT DANCER was running today. She got there a little early to settle in to calm her nerves. With a long dramatic stride, it only took her 10 paces to reach the stairwell. It was as if everything came to a halt to watch this performance. Both male and female stood still in reverence to her jaw-dropped beauty. These were the usual sights and sounds that was expected on opening day. Pure entertainment! Everyone in a synchronized flurry of color and motion scurrying to busy destinations.

The binocular vestibule was set between both staircases. Patrons would stop there to pick up their leather- cased binoculars that were stored throughout the racing season. Perky, the attendant handed her the box. Then she in return pulled out a ten spot and placed it kindly in his hand, "My quirky Perky, you are always looking slick. Enjoy your day. We have all twenty- four days ahead to savor in." He nodded in thanks and shyly smiled, as this was his demeanor. She flipped her hair back and strode right up the stairs not acknowledging any of the gawkers. Perky thought, "That loveable gal is quite the cuddle bunny. She sure knew how to make a damn entrance!" He put his head back down to dust off the vast rows of binoculars. The rest of the patrons continued their track rituals.

Lily, even with all her fan gawkers, was deeply lonely inside. This outward appearance of having an abundance of onlookers, ironically made her feel lonelier. It was oddly a silly sham she thought and made her feel detached rather than included from the conclave of gatherers. They were united in small groups of people having fun, laughing and talking, playing and being. She

*on the other hand was the essence of being completely
alone. Alone in her parade through the clubhouse. Alone
in her box sitting across from the finish line. Alone since
her early twenties, when her parents had died in a sudden
car accident up in the Adirondacks on a dark, rainy night
on Forest Home Road above Lake Placid. As a result,
leaving her to tend to the family's thoroughbred horse
business. Of course there were acquaintances, admirers,
and employees she came in contact with on the daily.
There were endless invitations often to social gatherings.
Through all of that she would put on a smile for them in
hope they did not see the truth of her lost existence. Her
self-imposed exile into herself was not a disconnect she
valued nor truly wanted, but one she somehow inherited.
It brought a profound state of isolation even in a crowd
as big as this at the racetrack on opening day. By
appearances she looked all put together. Yet somehow
she hid it with grace and dignity. Somehow this was her
foible and her fake out, to hide in open spaces and
pretend to have it all in place. But truth have it, she was
falling apart inside. Luckily her saving grace was her
self-awareness of the situation. She knew who she was
and who she wasn't. This is how she survived. This is
where she drew gratitude from. And this what she
thanked God for every day. She knew how to carry on.
That was her saving refuge.*

*And carry on she did right there with the crowd
directly in front of her view. They hurriedly proceeded to*

their spots along the rail. Grabbing coveted spots early was a ritual of this track bunch, to get ready to watch the first race on this special racing day. While others were devotedly out in the Paddock horse area four people deep, just to glimpse their favorite horse being readied for saddling. Jockeys and trainers were in close up, head to head quiet discussion on the strategy for the race. All with one common goal, to watch this honored, respected equine sport

The bugler was getting in place to ring out to ready the horses and jockeys to enter the track. The familiar sound that calls out to all jockeys to mount their horses. They began lining up near the paddock saddling area, from under the trees, for the first race of the season. Owners began their own rituals of getting ready to follow. Excitement was in the air. The fans were ecstatic. This moment had been long in the making. This horsey set was ready for it.

The beautiful chestnut stallion, Assault had just come off winning The Triple Crown, so a lot of racing experts were talking the talk about that rare fete. But the first race on today's card was what the current chatter from racing patrons was excitedly about. The common thread conversations at racetracks was always the race at hand: Who do you like this race? Which horses are the speed horses? What horse likes to come from behind? What trainer or jockey has the best record? For this start of the card, Big Sun and Lady Apple didn't have the best speed record but had the best names. Somehow this was the appeal to the majority of chalk bettors. Names were essential in keeping this type of bettor happy dappy. Boy Angler was a 5-2 shot on the morning line and seemed to be where most of the handicapper bets were hedging. Midnight Dancer was the beauty filly in the race, reminiscent of the Black Beauty and that is who the sentimental bettors were running to the mutual betting windows for, to lay down a few dollars. Lily owned this spectacular stunner and she was just getting ready to go into the Paddock area to watch her saddle. She almost couldn't catch her breath as she reached the saddle pavilion at the sight of this magnificent creature. The tips of her dark shiny mane blowing in the summer wind she saw from a distance as the sun was hitting the filly's face, reflecting off the reigns. Lily whispered into Midnight Dancer's ear, "Shine bright, sweet girl." That was the same words her Mom would whisper in her ear as a young girl to lift her up, "Shine bright, Lily White." And shine bright this filly did. Lilly prayed, "Beauty girl, let's make this happen," with fingers crossed.

The horses saddled as "Rider's up!" was heard. Jockeys mounted their respective horses. One behind the other, in numbered order, the parade of horses started the regimented march through the paddock. Year after year, season after season, racetrack after racetrack, somehow this tradition never lost its celebratory feel. Each and every race the excitement of the sport seeped

*into the souls of these fans. The onlookers along the path
cheered on their beloved horse or favorite jockey. This
pageantry is what made Saratoga Racetrack so magical.
This ceremony of cherished devotion is what brought fans
back every summer. The gallant majesty of the horses and
the muted colors of jockey silks from the stable colors
heading towards the historic track was set in motion to
bring this parade onto the dirt of the main track in front
of the clubhouse and grandstand. Adding to the regency,
this day was one of honored significance. Opening day
was always a celebration but today meant even more. The
closure for three years had taken the spirit from the town.
This significant race, this first race was bringing it back.
And the fans were grateful. You could feel it in the air.
You could see it in their eyes. And you could hear it in the
deafening roar of the crowd. The horses stepped onto this
venerable groomed dirt track and the proclamations of
booming cries of joy seemed to be a metaphor for the
town roaring back to life. This was it. This was the
moment they had been waiting for. A moment for the
history books. A genuine unity of connection.*

*Lily followed the post parade of horses from behind
with all the other owners and trainers rushing to get to
their seats or to the rail. She ran up the clubhouse stairs
with full on tummy tingles to the crowded, cramped
wooden boxes situated along the front row near the finish
line to get ready for her beloved filly. Drew Guiffre and
his beautiful lady Alexandria Coxwald, along with his*

*sassy sister Mimi Guiffre and her intellectual guy,
Leonard Valvano, sat a few boxes down the line from
Lily. They were still waiting on the whereabouts of Nicky
B. "Where was he? What was he up to?" was at the
center of their conversation over a bucket of ice cold
beers! They needed him to get this party started in full
motion. Without him, it was only half a party. Drew and
Lenny were in deep conversation as to why Nicky left so
abruptly Saturday night from The Worden Hotel bar.
They were still putting together oddly hypothesized
scenarios for what may have happened. They didn't want
to worry the girls. The ladies were in champagne cheers
mode trying to figure out their tote tickets for this race.
Both Mimi and Alexandria noticed the lady in white a few
boxes down from them. Fashionable ladies always
noticed other designer dressed fashionable ladies as if it
was a secret code. They kept notes in their mind files for
what to shop for on future shopping adventures.
Inspiration of interesting items. The unspoken solidarity
of womanhood. This day was exceptionally one of
fashion frolicking. And all the ladies were on each
other's couture radar.*

*As Lily sat alone, she noticed a glare coming from the
infield. The motionless pond out in the middle, on the
other side of the inner track, there floated a single canoe.
The iconic canoe that no one knew nor inquired about
where it had originated from. One of the sportswriters,
Peerless McGrath thought, "The famous blue canoe is
there which according to legend, provides transportation*

*for bettors who guess wrong back to the metropolitan
track at the end of the season, by way of the Hudson
River." Famed sports reporter, Red Smith said, "There
is, as there always has been, a blue canoe riding on the
lake with no one in it and no one to explain why it's
there." So there it was the canoe just floating and no one
knowing why. The sun kept reflecting off something in
the water that caught her eye. It was happily distracting
her, at the very least, from her nerves of anticipation for
the race ahead. Some kind of peace of mind came over
her as she watched the bouncing of the reflection. Lily
waved to Monty, Frank and Father Murphy who sat in
the the box behind her. Phil, her father's close friend,
gave a warm wave. He was the training morning's
racetrack clocker, a true handicapper, sprawled out in
his personal box which sat on the top row of cramped
boxes. A few other famous owners and trainers began to
walk by, readying to their seats and gave her the cordial
nod that blue bloods always gave each other at these
happenings. Somewhat like a knowing look of, "You are
accepted in our exclusive club of exclusivity." The same
club Lily wanted no part of. She loved the horses. She
loved the thrill of the sport. But she was not in love with
some of the pompous and affected self-importance that
flowed freely like the champagne she was just about to
order. This imbibe would help steady her for the
upcoming break open of the starting gate moment. Her
filly was itchy scratchy in the gate and the anticipated
moment was ready to happen. This entire group of horse*

fans was ready as they waited with bated breath. The announcer was ready. The horses were ready...

The track announcer yelled out, "And, they're off!" As he continued with the calling of the race,

"Big Sun and Slight Edge got the early jump from the rest of the field right out of the gate with a tiny edge. Boy Angler a close third as they hit the half mile pole. Big Sun takes the early lead.

Slight Edge had early speed but could not keep up, begins to weaken and falls back. Leaving Boy Angler and Big Sun to battle it out as they are approaching the stretch. Big Sun has forced the pace with a slight lead but is beginning to weaken. Boy Angler is now on his heels. Back and forth they go

The ladies are making their moves on the guys.

Lady Apple and Midnight Dancer are starting to gain ground on the inside. Midnight Dancer is hugging the rail as they come down the stretch. Boy Angler is a prominent threat rounding the stretch. All four horses are neck and neck.

The ladies are making the guys work.

With a furlong to run, Boy Angler picks up ground. Puts it into high gear and takes off nearing for home.

Boy Angler draws clear from the other three horses. Disposes of the pack in the stretch and roars into the lead. GO Angler GO! And that's how This Boy gets it done. Boy Angler wins the race by five lengths.

Lily was impressed with the courage of her Dancer keeping pace with the boys. She was overwhelmed with emotion. She was standing the entire time during this historic, thrilling race. As the formalities were taking place in the winner's circle, all eyes were on Boy Angler but her eyes were on another boy. As she looked across from the finish line and over to the pond, she saw a dark haired figure get out of the canoe. It was Nicky B. doing a long, dramatic stretch as if he had just woken up from a long nights sleep inside the canoe. He almost fell into the water as the canoe lost its balance but he managed to jump onto the infield grass with the agility of an athletic acrobat. Two swans normally indifferent to any of the horse action, fluttered their wings at this unordinary invasion of privacy. Lily started laughing out loud with such hysterical joy. Everyone nearby thought she was laughing in more of a hysterics fashion to cover up, for no apparent reason other than that filly had just lost this coveted race. Yet Lily felt all the past years stress disappear just from that one hilarious moment.

As Nicky jumped onto the grassy knoll, he looked over to the looming historical building and realized that the entire Clubhouse and Grandstand patrons were looking pointedly over at him. He looked side to side at his surroundings and realized where he was. He screamed out loudly, OHHHHHHHHH FUCK!" The group of onlookers burst out laughing with such force and intensity, the entire track shook to the wooden rafters from the high decibel of sound laughter. The track announcer was doing the same as he barely could get the words out, "Sir? Would you please vacate the canoe area and walk across the infield? Someone will escort you across the main track." The silliness of the situation registered in high hilarious mode. Not one person could contain their giggles and laughter.

As Nicky reached the winners circle, to go through the small gate near the jockeys weigh in station, he looked up and saw the beauty girl from last night at midnight on Lake Lonely. There she was shining down on him in white. He couldn't stop looking into her eyes. There was a kindness there saying, "You got this." He moved slowly, not looking away, he stopped and with a cool guy move, he bowed to her and did a thumbs up to her as if to say "I got this." Then his eyes caught Uncle Sallie's eyes. All Nicky could think was, "Why is Sallie's mouth wide open?" Then he saw his mother Mae, and gave her a hesitant little wave. With the sight of that wave and seeing him right in front of her, all Mae could do was breathe that sigh of relief a mother always feels when she knows her children are okay. She closed her eyes and whispered, "Thank God." Mae held up her glass of champagne with a nod and waved him to come up to the boxes. Nicky tucked his white rumpled shirt into his khaki pants. Ran his hand to brush his hair. He ran up the wooden steps, down the clubhouse aisle, and stopped in front of his Mom and Uncle with a sarcastic smirk only a 25 year old can pull off and get away with. Arms opened wide, ready for a hug. Then he received the Honored High Fives from his friends nearby as they handed him beers. Lily came by to join the fun.

All was right in the world as Nicky then settled in or was it? He looked over to Sallie and said something in his Uncle's ear after the crowd got back to business for the second race. Sallie looked puzzled as he tried taking it all in. A complete look of bewilderment came over his Uncle's face. The lightbulb had just went off for Nicky B. He had finally remembered. It came clear to him where the bookie's bag of cash was. Sal looked at him in a jaw dropped frenzy and before he could get out one word, Nicky began a full on sprint up the box area stairs back down the clubhouse stairs, through the betting window promenade, under the red awning, straight up through the Paddock and out onto the path to Union Avenue. Sal was chasing after him towards the direction of downtown. Nicky kept yelling over his shoulder, "I love you Uncle Sallie, you Big Bear." Almost tripping over the curb, Nicky yelled, "Hi De Ho!" in response to the happiness he was feeling. Passers-by were watching, stopping on sidewalks and drivers slowing down in cars, pausing to glance at this unusual, comedic spectacle. Sal was screaming out his usual silly, unintelligible salutations, puffing and sputtering, his hinges creaking and trying to

*catch his breath. He was yelling, "Can't you loop?
Can't you look? CANTALOUPE!", while shaking his fist
in the air, "You dumb fool. How could you have placed
the bag under the melons?!" Nicky thought to himself as
he looked behind him, "How lucky am I to have someone
with this much passion and gusto running after me."
With that clarity of resolution, he knew how much he
was loved by this big, befuddled, spirited and very
cantankerous man. This was a moment. He would take it.
He would keep it. And he would certainly with deep
regard, love him right back.*

Epilogue

As the sun was setting, the last race of the day had ended, the track goers were descending upon Union Avenue heading out towards the waters of Lake Lonely. Knowing the night would soon be upon them. Just being. Just sharing. Ready for some more connection. A mingling of tourists and natives all with one thing in mind, simply gathering so as not to be alone. Looking into the color of the dusk's summer night, knowing the season had just begun. This was their moment where they would start again… to make a joy.

Acknowledgments

I would like to thank a few people that were my true grit during the writing of my book.

Joseph. P. Tarantino, Sr., my grandfather, my inspiration for many of the historical stories within this story.

Bertha Mae LaDue, my grandmother, who was a single mother bringing up five children on her own, juggling two jobs, my inspiration for Mae's courage, strength and humor.

Wikepedia.org, is my go to encyclopedia for references. Please donate online to keep this free encyclopedia a resource: donate.wikimedia.org

Monty Wooley. Frank Sullivan, Dorothy Parker, Yaddo, Hawley Home, Saratoga Racetrack, Rileys Lake House, "Night and Day"- Film, Spuyten Duyvil, Van Raalte, Moe and Izzy, Cab Calloway Glossary of Jive Talk, "Stormy Weather" with Lena Horne, Chicago Club, Congress Theater, Worden Hotel, Colonial Tavern, Assault the horse, Captain Midnight, Ovaltine, Irish Poem, Prohibition, The Great Depression, WWII, Victory Garden, Algonquin and The Round Table, Carpathia, Cotton Club, "Saratoga Trunk"- Novel and Film, Edna Ferber, Max Steiner, "As Long As I Live"- the song, Studebaker.

National Museum of Racing for allowing me permission to resource the racing program reference from August 5, 1946.

Saratoga Springs History Museum, George Bolster Collection. Jamie Parillo, without you there would be no visual for the reader. You are a treasure to the preservation of our city's history.

Maryanne McLagan, my laugh a minute comrade, thank you for sharing your beloved father and North End stories.

Carol Cox., my blue larkspur inspire, you rock.

Peter Finley, third generation Saratogian, my friend and fellow writer, your words made it in.

Big Ron Solevo, your hilarious line from our dinner night with Nancy, Billy and I cannot still stop roaring with laughter.

Susan Lee Garrett, Elizabeth Macy, Jimmy Parker: true Saratoga Legacy Families, thank you for your heartfelt quotes.

Pam Cleveland, Billy Js right hand, thank you for letting me borrow you to become my right hand for a few days for the edit and making it look pretty.

Allie Cox, designer extraordinaire, your talent is soaring, your eye for design was the icing on the cake for the collaboration on the cover.

Thank you to Lenny Valvano for letting me use his exact name. The minute I met you, I knew that would be my favorite name but then you became one of my favorite people.

Billy Francis LeRoux, friends since grade school thank you for the trackside capture. You have the eye for art in photography.

To Debbi Wraga, a true treasure to writers and readers. I love our chats on edit moments. Two literary gals who talk at the same time but know what each other are saying. Northshire Bookstore is a gift that keeps on giving to our community.

To my friends and family, each and every one of you teach me something every day. For that, I am grateful. You are the fabric of my life-you know who you are.

My children Drew and Mia, you are my heart and soul.

My husband, Billy Jeffreys, you are my rock. I adore you.

Betting Windows Saratoga Racetrack, 1942

Photograph courtesy of the George S. Bolster Collection of the Saratoga Springs History Museum.

Worden Hotel Corner of Division Street and Broadway. 1945

*Photograph courtesy of the George S. Bolster Collection of the
Saratoga Springs History Museum.*

Worden Hotel Register Sign In, 1946

Photograph courtesy of the George S. Bolster Collection of the Saratoga Springs History Museum.

Model in Congress Park 1946 Clothing

Congress Theater on Broadway and Spring Street, 1946

*Photograph courtesy of the George S. Bolster Collection of the
Saratoga Springs History Museum.*

Clubhouse View, 1946

Photograph courtesy of the George S. Bolster Collection of the Saratoga Springs History Museum.

Colonial Tavern, 1946

Photograph courtesy of the George S. Bolster Collection of the Saratoga Springs History Museum.

Children's Party in 1946

Photograph courtesy of the George S. Bolster Collection of the Saratoga Springs History Museum.

Clubhouse Dining in 1947

Photograph courtesy of the George S. Bolster Collection of the Saratoga Springs History Museum.

Business Meeting in 1948

Photograph courtesy of the George S. Bolster Collection of the Saratoga Springs History Museum.

7

Monty Woolley with Trophy Racetrack Winner's Circle

Photograph courtesy of the George S. Bolster Collection of the Saratoga Springs History Museum.

Worden Hotel Bar, 1945

*Photograph courtesy of the George S. Bolster Collection of the
Saratoga Springs History Museum.*

Riley's Lakehouse, 1934

Photograph courtesy of the George S. Bolster Collection of the Saratoga Springs History Museum.

Saddling Shed, 1935

*Photograph courtesy of the George S. Bolster Collection of the
Saratoga Springs History Museum.*

Vicinity of Division Street and Railroad Place, 1935

Photograph courtesy of the George S. Bolster Collection of the Saratoga Springs History Museum.

Earlier Exterior of Colonial Tavern, 1937

Photograph courtesy of the George S. Bolster Collection of the Saratoga Springs History Museum.

Trackside Dining, 1937

Photograph courtesy of the George S. Bolster Collection of the
Saratoga Springs History Museum.

Saratoga Racetrack Clubhouse Bar, 1940

Photograph courtesy of the George S. Bolster Collection of the
Saratoga Springs History Museum.

Paddock Walk, 1940

Photograph courtesy of the George S. Bolster Collection of the Saratoga Springs History Museum.

Exterior Saratoga Racetrack, 1946

Photograph courtesy of the George S. Bolster Collection of the
Saratoga Springs History Museum.

Saratoga Paddock View in 1949

Photograph courtesy of the George S. Bolster Collection of the Saratoga Springs History Museum.

Horse Arrival on Circular Street

Photograph courtesy of the George S. Bolster Collection of the Saratoga Springs History Museum.

Saratoga Racetrack View during WW2